This book is dedicated to the Knights and White families. Shermaine, Andre', Jerry, Shanita, Eli, and Gabby, thank you for making our European adventure one we will never forget.

PAYTON GOES TO
Paris

BY

SHAYLA MCGHEE AND PAYTON MCGHEE

ILLUSTRATED BY STEFFI STANLEY

Payton hopped off the school bus, skipped up the sidewalk, and ran into her house.

Today was the last day of school and the day before she and her family were traveling to Paris for their summer vacation.

Their bags were all packed. The only thing Payton needed to do in the morning was grab Cameron, her favorite stuffed cat, and head out the door.

"Payton! Payton!" her little brother, Christian, and little sister, Riley, shouted when they saw her come in. "Can you tell us about Paris?"

"Sure," she said, hugging them. "I'll tell you all about it after dinner."

That night, Payton read a book to them that had tons of facts about Paris.

"Paris is a city in the country of France," she read while pointing to a map in the book.

"French is the official language. So, if we want to say hello to someone, we say bonjour."

"Bonjour!" they repeated, practicing their greeting.

Just then, Mommy and Daddy came into the room.
"Time for bed. We have a busy day tomorrow."

Payton kissed her brother and sister goodnight and headed to her room. She could not wait until tomorrow.

The next day, they boarded their flight. They enjoyed talking to the flight attendants and meeting the captain once the plane landed.

They were even given pins with wings on them for being such great passengers.

After they dropped off their suitcases at the hotel, they visited the Louvre, a museum filled with historic artwork and sculptures from around the world.

Payton roared when she saw the Great Sphinx of Tanis,

smiled when she looked at the painting of the Mona Lisa,

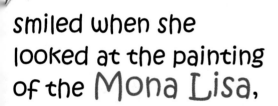

and posed next to the sculpture of Athena.

When they left the inside of the museum, they walked through the Tuileries Garden.

The merry-go-round ride was the favorite part of their stroll. "Hold on!" Payton called to her brother as they went around and around.

Next, they walked down the Champs-Élysées, a popular avenue in Paris that was filled with plenty of places to shop.

Mommy, Payton, and Riley decided to check out a fancy boutique that had pretty dresses in the store window.

As the girls tried them on, Payton imagined that they were walking down the runway in a Parisian fashion show.

After all, Paris is known for its great style.

With shopping bags in hand, they continued their walk down the avenue and arrived at the Arc de Triomphe.

The large monument was built to celebrate French victories of the past.

Payton examined its stone sculptures and visited the Tomb of the Unknown Soldier that lies underneath.

Their next destination was the Eiffel Tower.

On the way, they stopped at a cute little French bakery filled with pastries and confections. There were croissants, a flaky, buttery bread, small cakes that reminded her of seashells named madeleines, and tarts topped with fresh fruit.

Payton wanted to taste them all, but she decided to choose a small, round cookie with a tasty filling called a maCaron. "I could eat a dozen of these!" she exclaimed.

Finally, they reached the Eiffel Tower. They took pictures in front of the large iron structure before going to the top and looking out over the city.

Using one of the telescopes, she spotted the Jardins du Trocadéro and its magnificent fountain.

Afterward, they took a boat ride down the River Seine.

Their boat passed by the Notre Dame Cathedral. Payton tried really hard to see some of the gargoyles on the church's roof.

When they arrived back at the hotel, they ate dinner and began looking through the pictures they had taken throughout the day.

As the day turned to night, Mommy and Daddy called them to the balcony. "We have one more surprise for you. Close your eyes and count to three."

Payton, Riley, and Christian closed their eyes and counted. When they opened them, they were amazed to see that the Eiffel Tower was sparkling with glittery, bright lights in the distance.

Payton hugged her family as they watched together. She was truly grateful for this experience and could not wait to explore even more places around the world.

ABOUT THE AUTHORS

Shayla McGhee

Born and raised in Georgia, Shayla McGhee graduated Summa Cum Laude from Spelman College where she received her Bachelor of Arts in Political Science with a minor in Secondary Education. After completing her undergraduate studies, Shayla attended the University of Georgia School of Law and is a current member of the State Bar of Georgia. Her expertise in education afforded her the opportunity to create digital content for the state of Georgia. In addition to writing, she enjoys traveling and spending time with her family and friends. Find out more about Shayla and her family on Instagram @shaylatmcghee and @mcgheepartyof5.

Payton McGhee

Payton McGhee has a love for rainbows, unicorns, and of course, travel. In just a few short years, she has had the opportunity to visit Belgium, France, Holland, and England. When she is not writing in her journal, she can be found spending time with her family, playing with her friends, and participating in extra-curricular activities such as gymnastics and track. For more from Payton, subscribe to her YouTube channel, Payton's Playful Adventures.

www.sableinspiredbooks.com   **Facebook: @sableinspiredbooks**   **Instagram: @sableinspiredbooks**

Made in the USA
Middletown, DE
13 September 2021